The
Mysterious
Island

A Magical World Awaits You
Read

THE
SECRETS
OF
DROON

The Mysterious Island

by Tony Abbott
Illustrated by David Merrell
Cover illustration by Tim Jessell

SCHOLASTIC INC.
New York Toronto London Auckland Sydney
Mexico City New Delhi Hong Kong Buenos Aires

Book design by Dawn Adelman

ISBN-13: 978-0-590-10840-9
ISBN-10: 0-590-10840-9

36 35 34 33 32 31 30 29 28 27   9 10 11 12/0

Printed in the U.S.A.   40
First Scholastic printing, August 1999

To all children
who explore and dream
and imagine

Contents

One

The Storm

Keee-kkkk! Lightning crackled and flashed outside the windows of Eric Hinkle's basement.

But he and his friend Julie could only look at the soccer ball in the corner.

Boooom! The thunder two seconds later told them the storm was only a couple of miles away.

"Neal is going to freak out when he

sees," said Eric. Neal was Eric and Julie's friend.

Julie stared over his shoulder. "I'm freaking out already," she said. "Let's call him. His eyes will bug out. He's got to see this — now."

The two friends ran up the basement stairs to the kitchen. Eric picked up the telephone and punched in Neal's number. Another flash of lightning made the phone crackle in his ear.

"Hello, Neal?" Eric said when his friend answered. "You've got to come over right away."

"Are you kidding? There's going to be a humongous storm in five minutes," Neal replied. "Besides, I'm getting ready to eat. It's lunchtime."

"It's always lunchtime for you," Eric said. "Forget food, Neal. This is important."

Neal sighed. "It'd better be, for me to pass up one of my mom's tuna fish sandwiches. I'm coming."

After Neal hung up, Eric and Julie glanced out the window. The sky was getting very dark.

Eric began to smile. "Good day to hang out in my basement."

"You mean, hang out in Droon," Julie added.

Eric chuckled. "Of course that's what I mean."

In Eric's basement there was an entrance to another world.

A world that Eric, Julie, and Neal kept secret. The mysterious and magical world of Droon.

Droon was a place where a good wizard called Galen Longbeard and a young princess named Keeah battled a very evil sorcerer by the name of Lord Sparr.

Droon had all kinds of strange creatures, too. Galen's assistant, Max, was a spider troll, half spider, half troll. He could climb up anything and spin sticky webs with his eight long legs.

And then there were the Ninns. They were Lord Sparr's nasty, red-faced warriors who flew around on big lizards known as groggles.

And a witch named Demither. And —

Boom-ba-boom! The sky flashed outside, and thunder boomed just as the back door opened.

"Yikes!" Neal charged into the kitchen. "I think that storm followed me!"

Eric opened the basement door. "No time for talk. Everybody downstairs."

The moment they got to the bottom of the stairs — *kkkkk!* — the basement flashed white, and — *ba-boom!* — the walls rumbled, and — *splish!* — rain splashed hard against the house.

"*Hello*, storm," Julie said.

"All right," said Neal, stepping into the basement. "What is more important than tuna fish sandwiches?"

"That." Eric pointed to a corner of the basement. The soccer ball — Julie's soccer ball — was sitting on the workbench.

Actually, it was sitting *above* the workbench.

It was floating in the air.

"Whoa!" Neal gasped. "I repeat — whoa!"

"Not only that," Eric said. "You remember the first time we went to Droon and the soccer ball came with us and then it did that magical thing when we came back? Well, Julie and I were looking at it before, and —"

"Shhh!" Julie whispered. "It's doing it again!"

By the glow of the ceiling light they watched the ball begin to change.

The black and white patches moved slowly across the surface of the ball. The patches became the shapes of countries. And the ball itself became a globe of another world.

The world of Droon.

"It means we need to go," Julie said, looking at her two friends. "What else could it mean?"

"Last time, our dreams told us to go to Droon," Eric said. "But this is different. I think it's a sign from Keeah."

Neal took a deep breath. "What if something bad is happening? What if Lord Sparr is, like, attacking Keeah? Or Galen?"

Kaaa-kkkk! The room flashed white.

The lightbulb in the ceiling flickered and dimmed.

"There's only one way to find out," Eric said.

Doom-da-doom! Thunder exploded overhead.

"Hurry before the power goes," Julie added.

Eric felt his heart race as they went to the closet under the steps. Just like the other times, he pulled the door open and turned on the light.

They entered the small room.

Where are we going this time? Eric wondered.

So far, the stairs had never taken them to the same place twice. And the stairway always faded and reappeared in a new part of Droon.

That was just one of the secrets of Droon.

Julie shut the door behind them. Neal flicked off the light. The room was dark for an instant.

Then it wasn't.

Whoosh! The floor vanished, and a long flight of colored stairs shimmered into place.

"I love that!" said Eric.

A sudden, cold wind blew into their faces.

"Whoa!" Julie said. "Hold onto the railing."

"Hold your nose!" Neal said. "I smell fish!"

"Seawater!" said Eric. "The stairs are over an ocean or something. Maybe we should go back."

But even as he said that, it was too late.

Shloosh! — a huge wave of icy water splashed across the stairs.

Eric's feet slipped out from under him.

"Help!" He clutched for the railing. He missed.

"Eric!" Julie grasped his hand, but another wave followed the first. Eric slid off the stairs, pulling Julie with him. She grabbed for something to hold on to.

"That's my foot!" Neal yelled.

Neal slipped down, too.

Splish! Splash! Sploosh!

The three friends hit the water hard.

"Neal! Julie!" Eric cried.

Tall waves leaped and crashed around him.

"I'm here!" Julie shouted, gulping for air.

"Something's coming!" Neal yelled.

A dark shape plowed across the waves. It was the bow of a giant ship.

"Watch out for us!" Eric shouted.

But the ship charged toward them, faster and faster.

Two

Wings Over Water

Suddenly the ship slowed.

"Down sail!" boomed a deep voice above them. "Circle around! Drop a rope!"

Splash! A thick rope slapped the surface of the water. Eric, Neal, and Julie grabbed hold of the rope and climbed up.

The ship was huge, with red-and-yellow sails and blue wings that swept to the back.

As he climbed, Eric read the golden letters on the ship's side.

"The *Jaffa Wind*. Jaffa City is where Princess Keeah lives. This must be her boat!"

A strong hand reached down and helped them aboard.

"Our friends from the Upper World!" said a man in a long blue robe, smiling at them. It was Galen Longbeard, first wizard of Droon.

"You have come to us again," he said. "And again we can offer you nothing but danger."

"We had to come," Julie said. "The soccer ball turned into a globe of Droon. Did Keeah do that?"

"Eric! Julie! Neal!" cried Princess Keeah, running over. "You got my message. The magic must be working. I'm so happy to see you." She gave them all big hugs even though they were soaking wet.

"How can anyone be happy with *that* thing on board?" snapped Max. The spider troll's orange hair stood on end as he pointed to a small gold chest on the deck.

"Whoa," Neal said. "The Red Eye of Dawn is in there!"

The Red Eye of Dawn was a jewel of amazing power. Neal, Eric, and Julie had helped Keeah steal it from Lord Sparr's volcano palace.

"We're going to hide it in Jaffa City," said Keeah. "We can use your help. Then my father and I are going to search for my mother."

"You can count on us," said Eric.

A strange witch named Demither had told them that Keeah's mother was alive. But, like Demither herself, Queen Relna was under a curse.

Galen nodded. "But Sparr will do whatever he can to stop us. It is his angry heart that makes the Red Eye so dangerous. Come, we must hurry."

Ker-splash! Icy waves crashed against the sides of the ship as it gathered speed once again.

"With two wizards aboard we should be safe," Eric said, looking at Galen and Keeah.

"One and a half," Keeah said. "I've been practicing spells. But so far all I do is break things. Like this morning —"

Kkkk! A sudden bolt of lightning lit up the sky.

A dark swarm streaked across the clouds.

"Uh-oh," Neal said. "Unless I'm crazy, Lord Sparr has found us! And he's not alone!"

"Groggles!" Eric hissed. "Hundreds of them."

The sea bubbled suddenly like a cauldron. Waves splashed up higher and higher. Rain fell on the deck in big icy drops.

"Looks like he is bringing foul weather with him, too!" Max snapped. "Prepare for battle!"

The swarm of groggles flew low over the ship.

One of the flying lizards swooped down and landed on the deck. On its back was the evil sorcerer himself — Lord Sparr.

"Get away from my ship!" Keeah cried.

The sorcerer snarled as he slid off the groggle. His bald head gleamed. The fins behind his ears turned from purple to black. In his hand he held a long staff.

"Beware, Sparr," Galen boomed. "You are outnumbered."

"Right," said Julie. "And we're keeping the jewel! So you can forget about taking it."

Sparr's eyes flashed at the children.

"Ah, the magic stairs brought you again? When the Eye is mine, I'll climb those stairs to the Upper World!"

Eric shivered. *Sparr? In my world? My house?*

Without warning Sparr thrust his magic staff at the golden chest.

Ka-blam! The box blasted open, and a black armored glove tumbled across the deck. Fitted into the glove was the Red Eye of Dawn.

"You wicked creature!" Galen cried. "I will not let you have it!" He threw a sizzling bolt of blue light at Sparr. *Ka-koom!*

But Sparr's staff sucked up the light and threw it back at Galen.

Then the sorcerer grabbed the glove and slipped it on. Bright red light shot from its fingertips. "Your powers are weak, Galen. Now — Red Eye of Dawn, show me your power! Create for me a sea of fire!"

Ka-whoosh! A wall of fiery water rose up suddenly. The kids tumbled to the deck.

"Keeah!" yelled Eric. "Do a spell!"

"Break something big!" Julie cried. "Real big!"

Keeah struggled to her feet and aimed her fingers at the giant mast. *Bembo — switt!*

Suddenly — *crack!* — the towering mast split in half and fell toward Sparr.

Whoomf! Sparr was slammed back against the main cabin. The black glove was thrown from his hand.

"Yes!" Keeah shouted.

Galen leaped across the deck. Grabbing the glove, he flung it into the golden chest and held the lid down tight.

Sparr's face wrinkled in horror. "That power belongs to *me*! Rise, O Demither!"

"Demither?" Eric cried. "The witch?"

The waves thundered below. A huge

green serpent burst through the water. It had sawlike teeth, two powerful claws, and a long, spiky tail.

"The witch is a sea monster now!" Neal cried.

The serpent twisted her mighty tail around the ship and pulled tight.

Crack! The ship's planks began to break.

"The hull is splitting!" Max yelled out.

"And you will all drown!" Sparr howled, jumping back onto his groggle.

Keeah threw a thick rope to Julie. "Everyone hold tight!" Neal lunged and grabbed the rope.

"Eric," Keeah yelled. "Take the rope!"

"I can't reach it!" he cried.

The serpent witch lifted the ship high above the waves. She held it there for a moment and then threw it back down into the water.

Krrrrunch! The wooden hull shattered into shreds. And the *Jaffa Wind*, with everyone aboard, broke in two.

The ship sank instantly beneath the waves.

Three

Shipwrecked!

Eric's world went black and bubbly.

No! he thought. *This can't happen! I can't sink!*

He clawed at the icy water, trying to reach the surface. Then the waves opened above him. Eric lifted his head out of the water. His fingers felt something soft.

Was it . . . sand?

Yes! It was sand. Eric scrambled up

onto it. He sucked in a deep, deep breath. He opened his eyes.

He was on land, on a beach. He was alive.

"Julie! Neal! Keeah!" he called out.

No answer.

Eric looked to his left. All he saw was the beach stretching away until it curved out of sight. He looked to the right and saw the waves splashing against piles of rocks. Ahead of him was a thick jungle full of odd-shaped bushes and tall trees.

A dark haze hung over the treetops. The whole island was covered in fog.

"What *is* this place?" he said to himself.

Splursh! Another wave crashed against the nearby rocks. Something tumbled onto the sand.

Eric ran to the rocks. The waves had washed up some broken boards and a torn piece of cloth. They were from Keeah's ship.

Next to them, half covered by sand, was . . .

"The golden chest!" Eric gasped.

With the Eye, he knew, anything was possible. Maybe he could use it to find his friends. Maybe even to fight Sparr.

But where was Galen?

Where was everybody?

Carefully, Eric lifted the chest from the sand. He opened it. But instead of finding the black glove with the red stone, flames jumped up at him.

"Ahh!" Eric cried, nearly dropping the chest.

Suddenly the fire changed. Before his eyes the fire became hundreds of snaky creatures, slithering over one another.

They gleamed red, then silver, then red again. Sometimes they looked like flames. Sometimes they looked like rippling ropes of water.

"Don't eat us-s-s!" the creatures pleaded.

Eric set the chest carefully on the sand. "I'm not going to eat you. But . . . who are you?"

Many tiny silver heads twisted toward him.

"We are s-s-silfs. We have lived-d-d for centuries in the s-s-seas of Droon. Demither-r-r is our queen."

The sound the creatures made was more like singing than speaking. Their bubbly voices sounded as though they were talking underwater.

"Demither sank our ship," said Eric.

"Sparr has put a curse on her-r-r," one silf sang. "She must do things she doesn't want to-o-o. The Eye will give Sparr even more power-r-r."

Eric shook his head. "The Eye was lost at sea."

"No!" the silfs sang. "It is on this-s-s is-

land. This is one of Demither's-s-s many islands."

"The Eye is here?" Eric asked. "Where? I have to find it. I have to help Princess Keeah get it to Jaffa City."

Thwomp! Thwomp! A deep thumping sound came from down the beach.

"Hide," the silfs cried. "Ninns-s-s are coming!"

"Wait," Eric called out. "Help me find my friends. And tell me where the Eye is!"

"If we can-n-n help you, we will-l-l. . . ."

The creatures turned fiery red, then silver. Then they slid over the sand and away into the waves.

Thwomp! Dozens of heavy, red-faced warriors came marching slowly up the beach.

"Ninns!" Eric gasped. "I am out of here!"

Eric ran quickly into the thick jungle.

Strange and wild plants slapped him in the face as he raced. Slippery yellow vines coiled down from above and dangled in the paths.

The Ninns' thumping got louder.

Eric ran faster.

Suddenly the ground turned soft beneath him.

"Huh?" He stumbled and fell.

Fwit! A sticky web surrounded Eric like a sack. It pulled tight around him.

He couldn't get out. Then the sack — with Eric inside — flew into the air. It went up high into the yellow trees.

"Please, no!" he yelled. "Help, I'm trapped!"

He couldn't escape.

Thwomp! Thwomp! The Ninns marched closer.

Four

Trapped . . . with Friends

Eric pushed and pulled as hard as he could to break out of the sack. The more he struggled, the more he got tangled in its sticky web.

"Get me out of here!" he cried.

And still he was pulled higher into the yellow trees.

"Stop making so much noise!" hissed a voice from above. "Do you want the whole Ninn army to hear you?"

Eric stopped going up. The sack swung back and forth from a high branch. A branch someone was sitting on. "Kee-ah?"

The princess smiled at him. "And Max, too."

"Of course!" Max chirped from the branch above. "Who do you think spun this little trap?"

"Boy, am I glad to see you," Eric said. He told them quickly about the silfs.

"I've heard of the silfs, but I've never seen them," said Keeah.

"They told me the Red Eye is on this island," said Eric. "We need to find it."

Thwomp! Thwomp! The Ninns crossed the beach and marched into the jungle right below them.

"Galen is on the island, too," Keeah said. "But, look —"

In the middle of the troop of Ninns was

the wizard, wrapped from head to foot in thick chains.

Galen was their prisoner!

"My poor master!" Max whimpered.

One of the red-faced warriors below held up his six-fingered claw. "Sparr said wait here."

"He wants the old man alive," said another.

"For now, at least!" a third said, laughing.

The laughter reminded Eric of gargling.

A cold wind blew through the trees.

Keeah gritted her teeth as she looked up. "Sparr is coming!" she snarled.

A groggle landed on the ground. Lord Sparr slid off its back. He pointed his magic staff at Galen. "You know where the Eye is. Tell me."

Galen stared at Sparr. "Never. You may

put me in chains. But the children are brave and clever. They will trick you."

"Demither's island has many dangers," Sparr said. "Anything can happen. In the end, the Eye will be mine."

Galen struggled against his chains. "The children will find the jewel."

A thin smile broke across Sparr's lips. "And they will give it to me, *if* they want you to live. If I find it, it's mine. If they find it, it's also mine. Either way, I win."

Galen shook his head sadly. "You were not always so evil, Sparr!"

The sorcerer turned to the Ninns. "Take the wizard to the white cliff. Wait for my orders."

"At once, Lord Sparr," the head Ninn said.

Then Sparr waved his hand and spoke a strange word. The whole troop of Ninns, along with Galen, vanished.

"Oh, no!" Max whispered. "How will we find my master now?"

Keeah put her finger to her lips as Sparr began to laugh.

"Galen's 'brave' children will never get off this island alive!"

Sparr jumped onto his groggle, kicked once, and flew away. As he did, the thick, dark mist all over the island seemed to grow thicker and darker.

"Never get off this island alive?" Eric snarled. "Ha!"

Then he gulped. "We will, won't we?"

"Yes, if we find my master," Max said. "And when we do, I will kick Sparr with each of my eight legs!" Then he quickly spun a strong rope of spider silk, and they all slid to the ground.

Eric waved at the thick haze. "Now where do we go?"

"Yikes!" a voice screamed suddenly.

"Help us!" another voice screamed.

"I think that just answered my question!" Eric said.

"It's Julie and Neal!" Keeah said. "They're in the jungle. Let's go!"

They crashed through the thick trees as fast as they could. The long vines whipped against their faces. The bushes scratched them.

Suddenly they froze.

Julie and Neal were standing on a rock in the middle of a clearing.

Surrounding them were six nasty, icky, enormous —

"Bugs!" cried Max.

Five

Attack of the Icky Bugs

Sssss! The giant bugs hissed angrily at Neal. Their thick, pointed tongues lashed up at him.

"If one of those things licks me, I'm going to lose the lunch I never ate!" Neal shouted.

The bugs were hairy beetles about four feet long. Their hard brown shells gleamed like armor.

"Gross!" said Eric, ducking behind a tree.

"Eew!" said Keeah, jumping down beside him.

The bugs flicked their fuzzy legs at Neal and Julie. Their feelers twitched, and their tongues stuck out angrily.

"All I did was look at a rock," Neal said.

"It was an egg!" Julie shouted, pointing to a nearby pile of round pink eggs. "One of *their* eggs! And you didn't look, you touched!"

Neal shrugged. "So how do you say 'I'm sorry' in bug language?"

"If they even *have* a language," Max said. "The horrible creatures!"

Sssss! The bugs hissed and edged even closer.

Keeah turned to Eric and Max. "I'm going to try a spell. If it works, it will scare

the bugs for a few seconds. Then you two can help Neal and Julie escape."

"We will do it!" Max promised.

Keeah crossed her fingers. "Right, *if* I concentrate on something simple . . ."

Eric peered around the tree. "On the count of three, you guys run, okay?"

"How about on the count of one?" Neal asked.

"Very funny," Eric said. "One . . ."

Keeah jumped up. She pointed her hands at the bugs.

"Two . . ." said Eric.

Keeah narrowed her eyes. *"Tomba — snooka — jeeba —"*

". . . three!" Eric shouted.

"Three!" said Keeah. "No, wait! I mean *floo!*"

Too late. Neal and Julie were already leaping off the rock when — *ka-bam!* — a bolt of bright green light shot from Keeah's hands.

The air filled with smoke. The bugs shrieked — *eeee!* — and disappeared into the jungle.

Julie leaped over to the princess. "Keeah, you did it! Your incredible spell worked!"

Keeah stared at her hands. "I guess so. . . ."

Eric tried to wave away the smoke. "Where's Neal?"

"Here I am!" he yelled from behind them.

Julie and Eric turned around. Neal wasn't standing there. The only thing there was the pile of bug eggs.

"I hear him," Julie said, "but I don't see him."

"Hey, I'm right here!" Neal shouted again.

The pile of pink eggs moved. Out from underneath the pile popped a brown bug twice the size of a football. It had a hard, shiny shell, six thin legs with fuzz on them, three orange eyes, and two feelers sticking out from its head.

It was like all the other bugs only smaller.

A baby bug.

Eric staggered back. "Neal, is that . . . *you?*"

The brown bug scuttled across the pile of eggs and looked up at them. "Boy," the bug said in Neal's voice, "Keeah's spell made you sort of big, didn't it?"

Eric gulped. "The spell went wrong, all right," he began. "But . . . well, um, Neal, it's like, I mean —"

"You're a bug!" Julie shouted. "An icky icky bug!"

"The spider part of me resents that!" said Max.

"Oh, what have I done?" Keeah said. "Neal, I am *so* sorry!"

Neal rubbed his front legs together. Then he saw them and jumped. "Oh, man! This is not good. Change me back, Keeah. Change me back now!"

The princess stared at her fingertips and then back at Neal.

"You didn't answer right away!" Neal said. "You're supposed to say, 'Sure, Neal!' and do your zapping thing, and I'm *me* again." Neal closed his three eyes. "I'm ready. Go."

Keeah's own eyes welled up with tears. "I'm afraid to try."

Neal's fuzzy legs began to quiver, and his feelers twitched. "It's all a dream. It's all a dream. It's all a — hey, what's that?"

Suddenly he flicked his tongue at Julie's head.

"Eeeeeew!" she gasped, jerking backward.

"Sorry. There was a fly near you," Neal said. "At least it looked like a fly. It was yellow with bright green wings. Anyway, I missed it."

"What you saw was a Droonian seafly," Max said.

Suddenly Neal rubbed his legs together, making a strange, high-pitched sound.

Eric made a face. "Stop being such a bug."

"Shhh!" Neal hissed. He tilted his head and went still. "Say that again, please."

Eric blinked. "I said, stop being such a —"

"Not you!" Neal snapped. "The fly!"

Neal's big eyes flickered as the green-winged insect buzzed in a quick circle around his head. He kept nodding.

Eric turned to Keeah. "I don't hear anything."

Julie bit her lip. Then she brightened. "Maybe now that Neal is part insect he can understand the seafly language."

"I'm too much of a troll to understand it myself," said Max.

Soon there was a whole swarm of seaflies buzzing over them.

Neal scratched his head with his front legs. "They tell me that the groggles are nesting up there somewhere." He pointed up.

"Where there are groggles, there are Ninns," said Keeah. "And where there are Ninns —"

"There is my master, Galen!" Max chirped.

Julie looked up into the fog. "But

what's up there? It's too foggy to see anything."

Neal nodded and twitched his feelers a few times. The flies swarmed together in a dense, bright green lump. They began to buzz in ever-widening circles. Faster and faster they flew, around and around over the kids' heads, stirring up the air.

And as they did, the breeze they made began to clear away the dark fog.

Keeah looked up. "Oh, my gosh!" she gasped. "A mountain!"

Six

Groggle Mountain

Julie stared up. "You mean that was there the whole time?"

The mountain was steep and craggy. Its distant peak went through the clouds high above the island.

"It's awesome," said Eric. "I bet the white cliff is at the top. That's where Galen is being held prisoner."

"If Galen is at the top," Keeah said, "then to the top we're going! Max?"

"At once, my princess!" the spider troll replied. Then he began to spin his legs so quickly they seemed to blur. Moments later, he held a long coil of silky rope.

"Time to climb!" Max said.

"Just like gym class," Julie said.

Max and Neal leaped upward easily, tying the spider silk to rocks and ledges wherever they could.

"Last one up is a rotten bug egg!" Max squeaked, scurrying faster.

"Hey!" Neal complained, scrambling after him.

Keeah smiled, tightened her belt, grasped the rope, and pulled herself up. "Better hurry."

Without wasting a second more, Eric and Julie began their climb.

Strong winds battered them as they climbed higher and higher. They reached

one ledge after another without stopping. There wasn't time.

Soon they lost sight of the beach below.

"Careful," Julie said, joining Neal, Max, and Keeah on a narrow ledge. "Remember what the flies said. The groggles are up here. That means the Ninns are close by. They're not exactly going to welcome us."

"We're heading into danger," Keeah added.

Eric's heart raced. He stopped to catch his breath. "Why are the tiny creatures friendly and the big, powerful ones mean? Answer me that."

Neal, clinging to the ledge above, turned. "Size has *nothing* to do with power," he said.

Keeah smiled. "Let me guess, the flies told you that?"

"Nope. I made it up myself," said Neal

with a chuckle. "It must be the bug in me talking."

Kaww! Kaww!

Sudden cries echoed down the mountain.

"Groggles!" Keeah shouted. "Take cover!"

Everyone huddled under the ledge.

Everyone except Eric. He tried to pull himself up to where the others were. "Wait for me!"

But the groggles wouldn't wait. With a loud flapping noise, two of the big flying lizards swooped out of the sky, spotted Eric, and dived right for him.

"Go away, you ugly creeps!" Julie shouted. They all started pelting the groggles with rocks.

Kaww! Kaww!

One groggle shrieked, then pulled away.

But the second circled around for Eric again.

"Leave me alone!" Eric yelled, flailing his arms.

"More rocks!" Max cried, tossing handfuls of stones at the beast.

But the groggle kept dodging them.

Its sharp claws dug and scratched at one end of the ledge Eric was clinging to.

The rocks began to break away, tumbling down the mountain to the trees below.

"Oh, man!" Eric groaned. "Get me out of here!" He glanced to his left. The ledge narrowed to nothing only a few feet from him. On his right, the groggle was ripping the mountain away in huge clawfuls.

There was nowhere for him to go.

His friends kept throwing rocks at the beast.

"Hold on, Eric!" Neal shouted to him.

But Eric couldn't hold on.

There was nothing to hold onto.

Kaww! Kaww! The groggle lunged again.

The ledge crumbled away.

Eric grasped wildly at the air.

He fell.

Seven

The Glove of Power

"Nooooo!" Eric screamed.

The earth seemed to swoop up at him as he plummeted toward the jungle. In seconds he would crash into the treetops.

Suddenly something hard and bony wrapped around him. It tightened on his waist. It was a groggle's thick claw grasping him tight.

"Let me go!" Eric cried as the lizard

lifted him high into the air. "Well . . . I mean, don't actually let me go, but —"

Kaww! Kaww! the huge beast shrieked.

"— let me go!"

The groggle flapped quickly past Eric's friends. They yelled something out to him, but he couldn't hear what it was.

"Probably good-bye!" Eric groaned, twisting in the groggle's grip.

The beast soared up the mountain, then slowed and hovered over a broad, flat ridge.

Looking down, Eric could see a large mound of sticks and other junk in the middle of the ridge. The pile had a dip in the center.

"A nest!" he whispered to himself. "Please don't eat me!"

Kaww! The groggle swooped over the nest. It loosened its claws and dropped Eric.

"Oomph!" he groaned when he hit bottom. The groggle circled once, then flew off.

"Probably going to tell his friends that lunch is ready. Yeah? Well, no way!"

Eric scrambled to his feet. The thick nest surrounded him like a huge bowl. The walls of it, he figured, were about ten feet high. He could get out fairly easily.

"And I sure can't stay here!"

Eric dug his right foot in and hoisted himself up with his tired arms.

The nest was made of tangled branches and vines. In with them Eric noticed strips of polished wood and red-and-yellow cloth.

He knew what they were.

The remains of Keeah's ship.

"Robbers!" he snarled. Then he noticed something else. Something shiny and black. He stopped climbing. He peered down.

"The armored glove . . ." he whispered. He leaned into the branches, untangled the glove, and dragged it out. Carefully, he turned it over.

The setting for the jewel was broken.

The Red Eye of Dawn was not there.

Crack!

Eric froze. Sounds were coming from outside the nest. He crept up the rest of the way and peered over the top.

He laughed. He waved.

"Eric!" Neal squeaked, scrambling over the top of the ledge. The others followed close behind. Eric jumped from the nest and ran to meet them.

"We're safe," Keeah said, "but not for long. The groggles made such an incredible fuss that now the Ninns are coming."

"Oh, man!" Eric said. "Can't we ever get a break?"

Clomp! Clomp! A pack of fat Ninn soldiers hustled around the other side of the broad ledge.

"Guess not!" Neal yelped. "Yikes!"

Max squeaked. "May I suggest we go the opposite way?"

"You get my vote!" said Julie.

The heavy red warriors wasted no time, either.

They quickly loaded their bows.

"Aim!" one of them shouted.

"Yikes again!" Neal squeaked. "Duck everyone!"

"Fire!" the Ninns yelled.

Thwang! Thwang! Flaming arrows whizzed by the kids. They skidded along the ground and crashed against the rocks. The Ninns growled and reloaded.

"Hey, Ninns, let me give you a hand!" Eric shouted. He threw the armored glove right into the center of the pack of Ninns.

The fat warriors paused to look at it.

"And we're out of here!" Julie yelled.

The kids dashed around the nest to the far side of the ledge. Max shot in front, scampering as quickly as his eight legs could carry him. Neal raced right behind him.

They circled around the side of the mountain.

"A cave!" Neal said. "I see a cave!"

"I saw it first!" Max chirped.

They all leaped through the mouth of the cave and ran inside. They dashed into the shadows and held their breath.

Max held up one of his legs. "Listen. The Ninns aren't following. We've lost them."

"I think there's a reason," Julie whispered.

Eric turned to look. "Oh, man!" he groaned. "Isn't there at least *one* place on this island that isn't dangerous?"

Coming out of the cave depths were several large fuzzy legs and long twitching feelers.

"Here we go again," Neal said with a sigh.

Sssss!

Eight

Cave of Bugs

Ssss! Ssss!

The kids huddled in the shadows as two large brown-shelled bugs clambered out from the back of the cave.

"Your family, Neal," Julie whispered.

The bugs hissed and groaned. Their feelers twitched in the air. Then the kids saw why.

In the thin light streaming from the cave's opening, they saw a giant pit.

A giant pit full of eggs.

Julie sighed. "Been there, done that."

Sssss! The bugs hissed again more loudly than before. Their tongues flicked at the eggs.

"Listen, people," Neal whispered. "The bugs don't see us yet. Maybe we should just fight the Ninns, one on one."

"Ten on one, you mean," Max chittered.

"Holy cow," said Eric. "There it is!"

He pointed to the pit full of round pink eggs. One egg was smaller than the rest.

It was shiny.

It glowed bright red.

And it was shooting off sparks.

"The Red Eye of Dawn!" Keeah whispered. "My gosh! We found it!"

The bugs circled the pit, hissing and flicking.

Julie bit her lip. "Can't they tell the

glowing red one with all the sparks is not an egg?"

"They're bugs," Neal snorted. "They aren't that smart. Believe me, I know."

The red jewel sparkled again.

"Now I'm sorry I threw the glove away," Eric said. "How are we even going to touch that thing? It'll burn us for sure."

Keeah shook her head slowly. "Maybe there's a way. Galen said it was Sparr's anger that makes the Eye dangerous."

Neal's three eyes stared at the Eye. "And that means . . . ?"

"I know," said Julie. "It's like, if *you're* angry, the *Eye* is angry."

Eric nodded. "And maybe if you're the opposite of angry, the Eye won't shoot those deadly red beams everywhere."

"What's the opposite of angry?" Neal asked. "Being happy? Like laughing and stuff?"

Sssss! The bugs hissed and flicked again.

"That's the problem," Keeah whispered. "I don't feel happy. I just feel scared."

Julie turned to Neal. "Do bugs get scared?"

"Don't look at me," he replied. "I've been blasted once already. Besides, you definitely do *not* want to smell fried insect."

"No, it's my job," said Keeah. "I'm a wizard, sort of, halfway, at least."

"But how will you get past *them*?" Max said, nodding toward the bugs.

Julie held up her finger. "Wait, I have a plan."

"What plan?" Eric asked.

"The one where Neal pretends to be their baby bug. You know, to distract them."

Neal backed up as far as he could. "I

don't think so! I may be a dumb insect, but I'm not *that* dumb!"

"But, Neal," whispered Julie, "they'll be so excited to see you, Keeah can grab the jewel. It'll be perfect."

"Perfectly nuts!" Neal grumbled. "They'll lick me with those creepy tongues! No way!"

"We need the Eye to help free Galen," Keeah said. "Only Galen can make you yourself again."

Neal was quiet. His feelers twitched and quivered. He cleared his throat with a tiny cough. "Myself again? Really?"

"Plus, it'll be funny," said Eric. "Keeah will laugh so we won't blow up."

Neal sighed. "I guess so. But next time, someone else can be the bug!"

He fluttered his feelers once, took a squeaky breath, then scuttled out of the shadows.

"Mama! Papa!" he cried. "I'm home!"

The big bugs swung around, opened their feelers wide, and lunged for Neal. *Yeeeee!*

Keeah laughed as she scurried to the eggs.

The bugs completely surrounded Neal, squealing with delight.

"Hurry!" Neal yelled. "They're licking!"

Keeah laughed harder. Her hands closed firmly around the glowing red jewel.

"She's got it!" Max chirped. "And it's not shooting red bolts!"

"Neal," Eric cried. "Get out of there!"

In a flash, the five friends dashed out of the cave. The bugs hissed and squealed, but the kids shot around the ledge and up the side of the mountain before they could catch up.

Higher and higher they went, until there wasn't any more mountain to climb.

They crawled over the last rise.

A sharp wind passed over them.

They found themselves standing under a dark, open sky.

They were on the edge of a white cliff overlooking the vast sea of Droon.

Galen was there, wrapped in chains.

A hundred Ninns were there, guarding him.

And Lord Sparr was there, too.

"Give me the jewel . . . or die!" he snarled.

"Uh . . . is there a third choice?" Neal asked.

At once — *whoom!* — a wall of raging flames shot up around the kids.

"Trapped again," said Eric.

Nine

At the White Cliff

The kids huddled together to avoid the flames.

"A prison of fire," Sparr said. "You may thank Witch Demither for the idea. Thoughtful, isn't she?"

"My happy mood is fading fast," Keeah whispered. The wall of fire edged closer.

"Let them go," Galen boomed, struggling against his chains.

"Give me the Eye and you may all go,"

Sparr told them. He snapped his fingers, and one large Ninn raised his heavy sword. "Your chains will be cut, Galen. You will be free."

Max's eight legs trembled. "D-d-don't trust him."

Eric looked up. The flames coiled high into the air. The strange, green-winged sea-flies were beginning to gather above them.

Eric felt something wasn't right.

What was it?

Sparr stared through the flames. "I created the Red Eye of Dawn centuries ago to do my will —"

"Your evil will!" Keeah said, trying to remain calm. "All you do is put curses on people. Like Demither. Like my mother!"

Eric kept staring at their prison of fire. Demither's fire. He recalled how she had said once that she was a friend to no one, not even to Sparr.

The flames slithered over one another. They gleamed red, then silver, then red again. The Ninns were afraid of the fire. They wouldn't come close.

But still, something was wrong.

Zzzz! The seaflies buzzed lower.

Then, in a flash, Eric knew what it was. The fire looked hot enough to burn them to a crisp. But no smoke was coming from the fire. And no heat. The flies would never buzz so close if there was heat. That was it! The fire wasn't real.

It only *looked* hot.

The fire was . . . something else.

In fact, it was *hundreds* of something elses!

Sparr circled the flames. Soon, he would guess. Demither had tricked him.

In an instant, Eric formed a plan. He tapped Neal with his foot and glanced up at the seaflies. Then he nodded at the Ninn with the sword. "Can your pals do something?"

Neal smiled a big smile. He twitched his feelers. Slowly, the flies lifted and buzzed over to the Ninn.

"Give me the Eye!" Sparr demanded.

"Get ready to move," Eric whispered. He stepped to the wall of fire.

"Eric, what are you doing?" Julie said.

"Just follow me." He held out his hand.

"Master Eric, no!" cried Max.

"Now!" Eric shouted.

Neal twitched, and the flies surrounded the fat Ninn. "Ugh!" the guard growled, swatting the flies. His heavy sword dropped to the ground.

At the same instant, Eric leaped through the fire. He was ready to scream, but he didn't have to. The instant he stuck his hand in, the flames ran over his fingers. The fire was icy cold!

"Silfs! I knew it!" he cried. The strange creatures spilled in a shower to the ground.

"Demither has betrayed me!" Sparr cried.

Eric and Julie dashed over and grabbed the Ninn's sword. Together they swung hard.

Chung! Galen's heavy chains fell away.

"Now you will pay!" Sparr shouted.

"No, Sparr," Keeah cried. "You will pay for the curses you have put on people!"

Ka-whoom! Bright beams shot wildly from Keeah's hand.

A terrible bolt blasted the ground near the Ninns, sending them rushing in every direction.

Another exploded near Neal.

"Oww!" he cried, as he leaped for cover.

"Keeah!" Galen shouted. "You cannot

control the Eye. Your anger will destroy you!"

"Throw it away!" Max yelled.

Keeah hurled the burning stone at the sea.

"IT IS MINE!" Sparr cried. He sucked in his breath and seemed to grow to twice his size. His eyes flashed, and his fins turned black with rage. He grasped his magic staff.

Ka-bam! Bolts of fire leaped from the staff. They shot across the air to the Eye. And the jewel stopped its fall to the sea. Slowly, it moved back toward Sparr.

"You see? The Red Eye of Dawn knows its master!" he howled. "Come to me, my jewel!"

Laughing, he reached for the sparking jewel.

Suddenly — *KA-WHOOOM!*

The peaceful sea exploded, and a giant serpent rose from the waves.

"Witch Demither!" Eric said.

The serpent reared her head and opened her jaws. "I am Demither, queen of oceans!"

And with a single lunge of her scaly arm, the witch closed her claws over the Red Eye of Dawn.

"No!" Sparr cried out. "Black was the day you were born, Witch Demither! I will find you!"

The serpent reared once more, then plunged into the water below, sending up a wave that crashed against the cliff like an exploding bomb.

"Awesome!" Julie gasped, staring at the water.

The sorcerer leaped upon a groggle and soared over the white cliff. "Ninns, follow me!"

Then, turning to Eric and his friends, Sparr cried, "Weak humans! You will end your days on this island! Crumble, earth! Fall to the sea!"

And the ground began to quake.

Ten

A Ship Reborn

Kaww! Kaww! The entire army of Ninns streaked across the sky after Lord Sparr.

The whole island rumbled and shook. Giant cracks split the rocks along the cliff.

"Let's get out of here!" Neal yelled, stumbling across the ground to his friends.

Eric gasped when he saw his friend. "Hey, Neal, you're back!"

"What's wrong with my back?" Neal said.

"It's normal!" Julie said. "You're Neal again! Not a bug! The Eye must have blasted you back to your regular you!"

"I always did like me!" Neal said. "Let's go!"

Rrrrr! The ground rumbled again and again.

"This way!" Galen urged. "The island is crumbling into the sea! Swiftly now!"

The six friends ran as quickly as they could down the white cliffs. They pounded through the tangled jungle. Rocks slid and crashed all around them. Trees fell in their path.

Finally, they reached the shore.

Krrrk! The giant white cliff above them began to split.

"We need a ship!" Keeah said.

Galen frowned. "We need something to

start us off. Something to build a ship with."

Eric's eyes went wide. "I know!" He ran across the beach. There, hidden in the rocks, were the wooden planks and torn sail from the old ship.

"Can we use these?" he asked breathlessly.

"Yes!" said Keeah.

Quickly, they assembled as much of the old ship as they could find. Together Galen and Keeah spoke fantastic words over them.

Suddenly, magically, the broken planks became hundreds of planks. Torn bits of sail furled upward into red-and-yellow squares of cloth.

The *Jaffa Wind*, more beautiful than ever, rose up before them.

"Hurry aboard," Max pleaded.

The moment they piled on, the giant

sails filled with wind, and the ship began to slide over the water.

KRRRK! A large crack tore open the cliff face, sending huge rocks tumbling to the sea below.

"Just in time!" Eric said.

The beach and the jungle were swept away by the crashing waves.

A moment later, the towering mountain itself fell into the sea. The mysterious island vanished.

As if it had never existed.

The ship sped magically over the waves.

Leaning against the side, Eric let out a long breath. "Sparr lost today," he said.

Keeah smiled. "Yes. For now, he doesn't have the Red Eye of Dawn. Now my father and I can search for my mother."

"What will Sparr do next?" Neal asked.

Galen glanced across the water. "Demither is heading north," he said, "to the coast of Mintar where she became what she became. Sparr will follow her there. But that is a story for another day. Look . . ."

The sun peered through the dark clouds and shone over the sea. It was a new day.

"And look at that," Neal said. "A city!"

They all ran to the upper deck. Rising in the distance were the silvery towers of an enormous city. Sunlight glimmered on the harbor and on the many colorful boats sailing into it.

"Jaffa City," Keeah exclaimed. "The capital of Droon. Home."

"We're home, too," Julie said. "There are the stairs." She pointed off the left side of the ship. The magic stairs were hovering over the calm waves.

A few minutes later, Neal, Julie, and Eric stepped from the ship onto the bottom stair.

"I have no words to thank you," Keeah said, "except to say — come back soon!"

"Droon needs such good friends as you," Galen said with a smile.

Eric smiled, too. "As long as the magic keeps working, we'll keep coming."

Julie hugged Keeah. "You can count on it."

"Farewell, Master Neal," said Max. "It was fun not being the smallest one, for a change."

Neal put his fingers to his forehead and wiggled twice. "That means — see you soon!"

The three children waved and raced up the stairs to the basement above them. They turned to look one last time at Keeah's ship as it sped over the sparkling sea to Jaffa City.

Then Eric flicked on the light.

Whoosh! The stairs vanished below them, and the gray cement floor appeared in its place.

"That was so strange," Eric said.

"The weirdest ever," Neal agreed.

They entered the basement.

Julie sighed. "But, somehow, I can't wait until we go again."

"Me, either," said Eric. "I wonder where we'll be next time. Jaffa City? The coast of Mintar?"

Neal made a face. "As long as they don't have bugs! Anyway, as Galen said, that's a story for another day. Look."

The soccer ball was lying on the work-bench.

It was a normal ball once again.

Light flashed in through the basement windows. But it wasn't lightning. It was the sun.

"The storm's over," Eric said. Then he turned to his friends. "Anybody hungry?"

Neal grinned and twitched his fingers. "That means — you better believe it!"

Then they all ran up to the kitchen for lunch.

ABOUT THE AUTHOR

Tony Abbott is the author of more than two dozen funny novels for young readers, including the popular *Danger Guys* books and *The Weird Zone* series. Since childhood he has been drawn to stories that challenge the imagination, and, like Eric, Julie, and Neal, he often dreamed of finding doors that open to other worlds. Now that he is older — though not quite as old as Galen Longbeard — he believes he may have found some of those doors. They are called books. Tony Abbott was born in Ohio and now lives with his wife and two daughters in Connecticut.

Under the stairs, a magical world awaits you!

THE SECRETS OF DROON

A New Series by Tony Abbott

The world of Droon is a
magical and beautiful place.
But it's a place where all is not well.

Eric and his friends have discovered
the door to Droon. Now the real
adventure is about to begin!

Look for

The Secrets of Droon:

**#1: *The Hidden Stairs and
the Magic Carpet***

#2: *Journey to the Volcano Palace*

Available at bookstores everywhere!